Dear Parent:
Your child's love of reading starts here!

Every child learns to read in a different way and at his or her own speed. Some go back and forth between reading levels and read favorite books again and again. Others read through each level in order. You can help your young reader improve and become more confident by encouraging his or her own interests and abilities. From books your child reads with you to the first books he or she reads alone, there are I Can Read Books for every stage of reading:

SHARED READING
Basic language, word repetition, and whimsical illustrations, ideal for sharing with your emergent reader

BEGINNING READING
Short sentences, familiar words, and simple concepts for children eager to read on their own

READING WITH HELP
Engaging stories, longer sentences, and language play for developing readers

READING ALONE
Complex plots, challenging vocabulary, and high-interest topics for the independent reader

I Can Read Books have introduced children to the joy of reading since 1957. Featuring award-winning authors and illustrators and a fabulous cast of beloved characters, I Can Read Books set the standard for beginning readers.

A lifetime of discovery begins wi'   Read!"

Visit www.icanreac
on enriching your chi

I Can Read® and I Can Read Book® are trademarks of HarperCollins Publishers.

Harry's Squirrel Trouble
Text copyright © 2022 by The Estate of Gene Zion
Illustrations copyright © 2022 by Wendy Graham Sherwood, Mindy Menschell, and Phillip Clendaniel

Library of Congress Control Number: 2021948186
ISBN 978-0-06-274775-4 (trade bdg.) — ISBN 978-0-06-274774-7 (pbk)

The artist used Adobe Photoshop to create the digital illustrations for this book.

22 23 24 25 26   LSCC   10 9 8 7 6 5 4 3 2 1   ❖   First Edition

HARRY'S
Squirrel Trouble

Based on the character created by
Gene Zion and Margaret Bloy Graham

by Laura Driscoll and pictures by Saba Joshaghani
in the styles of Gene Zion and Margaret Bloy Graham

HARPER
An Imprint of HarperCollinsPublishers

Harry was a white dog

with black spots.

He liked everything,

except the squirrel in the backyard.

The squirrel chewed the table.

She dug holes in the grass.

The squirrel bit off the flowers.

The squirrel did all those things.

But the children blamed Harry.

Harry did not like

getting in trouble.

Suddenly Harry had an idea.

He would be a watchdog.

He would stop that squirrel!

Harry watched the squirrel

on the clothesline.

She grabbed a sock.

Harry jumped up on the table.

He grabbed the other end of the sock.

It was a tug-of-war!

At last, the squirrel let go.

She ran up the tree.

"Hooray!" thought Harry.

But then . . .

"Harry!" said the little boy.

"Leave the clothes alone!"

Harry barked.

But the boy did not understand

what Harry was saying.

The next day, the squirrel ran
into the garden.
She chomped on a tomato—
the biggest, reddest one.
Harry barked.
The squirrel ran away.

"Harry!" said the little girl.

"Leave the tomatoes alone!

Time for you to come inside."

Harry watched the squirrel

nibble more and more tomatoes.

He barked and barked.

"Too loud!" said the little boy.

"No more barking!"

"Not fair!" thought Harry.

That squirrel made all the trouble.

But Harry got all the blame.

The next day,

the family turned on the sprinkler.

It made a big puddle.

That gave Harry a new idea!

Harry dragged the sprinkler

to the bottom of the tree.

The ground got wet and muddy.

Then Harry watched and waited.

The squirrel came down the tree.

She ran through the mud.

She jumped onto the doghouse.

She ran across the clean sheet.

The squirrel dashed back up the tree
just when the back door opened.
The children ran outside to play.

"Oh no!" said the little girl.

She pointed at the doghouse.

There were muddy tracks

all over the roof.

23

"Oh, Harry!" said the little boy.

"Wait!" said the little girl.

"Harry did NOT do this.

These are not dog tracks.

They are too little."

Then Harry saw the squirrel.

He barked and barked

at the bottom of the tree.

The children looked up.

"Those are squirrel tracks!

That's why Harry keeps barking!"

said the little boy.

"Right, Harry?"

This time when Harry barked,

he wagged his tail.

The children looked at the flowers.

"That squirrel did this,"

said the little girl.

The children looked

at the holes in the grass.

"That squirrel dug these holes,"

said the little boy.

"It wasn't Harry after all."

Then Harry pointed to the garden.

The squirrel was about to bite

another big, red tomato.

The children shouted.

Harry barked.

The squirrel ran away.

"I'm sorry, Harry!"

the little boy said.

"I'm sorry, too!" said the little girl.

"We didn't understand

what you were trying to tell us."

Harry was so happy.

He loved his family.

He loved his backyard
and everything in it.

Maybe even that squirrel.